THE ROYAL HUNT

THE HUNT FOR PRINCE VESPIAN

Charlotte Schoff

authorHOUSE®

AuthorHouse™
1663 Liberty Drive
Bloomington, IN 47403
www.authorhouse.com
Phone: 833-262-8899

Published by AuthorHouse 01/07/2022

ISBN: 978-1-6655-4861-8 (sc)
ISBN: 978-1-6655-4860-1 (e)

THE ROYAL HUNT-THE HUNT FOR PRINCE VESPIAN

The Year- Fifteen and Ten
The Territory- Hollowfield
The Castle- Dragonshire
The Village- Edondale

The Players
The King- King Zandor
The Queen- Queen Callie
The Princess- Princess Galanthria
The Prince- Prince Vaspian
The Captain Of The Guards- Precious

The Hunting Party
Lord Of The Woods- Kendelyn (elvin- Kind)
Lady Of The Woods- Glendora (Elvin- Kind)
Lady Of The Lake- Fandora (Mer-Folk)
Dwarf male- Loren (Fighter)

Human Male- Malaki (Mage)
Half Elf Female_ Farteema (Tracker)
Half Elf Female- Veronna (Ranger)
Human male- Homri (illusionist)
Wizard Female- Arigwin (Wizard)

Place Of Worship- House Of The Angles On High

Prologue

The Royal Stage Coach is on its way to Castle Dragonshire, in the Territory of Hollowfield carrying some precious cargo by the name of Prince Vaspian.

Princess Galanthria, and Prince Vaspian were Betrothed at birth.

On the way to the castle, the stagecoach carrying Prince Vaspian was forced to stop. The driver of the coach fell to the ground and knocked unconscious by a gang of men. Prince Vaspian was kidnapped, and taken into the woods by six bandits.

Find out what happens to the Prince by reading the second installment of "The Royal Hunt-n The Hunt For Prince Vaspian.

Chapter 1

The Year is still Fifteen Ten, and King Zandor is still on the throne, with his lovely wife Queen Callie, and Princess Galanthria by his side.

Castle Dragonshire in the Territory of Hollowfield.

In the village of Edondale, is a small inn by the name of "The Wayward Inn" where the Hunting Party is bedding down, resting from rescuing Princess Galanthria from the evil witch, and her pet black dragon, to bring the Princess back to King Zandor, and her mother Callie, to take their place next to the King's side on the throne.

After the Hunting Party had checked into their rooms, they all went down to the restaurant at the inn to have a meal, and drink. They had rabbit, Mashed potatoes, green beans, and cornbread, with white wine to drink, and fruit pie for dessert.

The next morning the King had dispatched a messenger to discuss a Very important matter.

The next morning the Hunting Party made their

appearance in front of the King. King Zandor had news that when his daughter Princess Galanthria was born she was betrothed to Prince Vaspian of Eagleland.

The day finally came for the Prince to come here to Castle Dragonshire to be with his Princess, but yesterday I got word from his stage coach driver that the stage coach was stopped and the Prince was kidnapped by a group of six bandits.

The stagecoach driver is in the hospital.He said that he fell of the coach and hit his head and passed out, but before he passed out he heard the men say that they were taking the Prince to an underground city, to stand trial for the crimes committed on the public.

King Zandor told the Party that they were needed one more time to go on another quest, this time to find Prince Vaspian and bring him back to the Castle to Princess Galanthria

King Zandor told the Hunting Party that it was a tradition, that when a child of Royalty is born the parents decide whom he or she shall marry. Eagleland Hollonfield's allay, and the Prince and Princess were betrothed to each other. To marry on their sixteenth birthdays.

King Zandor said "Please Kendelyn, please find Prince Vaspian and bring him back alive.

Kendelyn told King Zandor that the Party would take on this quest. First off the Party needed to go back to the village, and gather up more supplies. Before the Party had left, they returned to the Castle, they told the Princess that they would find the Prince, and bring him back to her alive.

The Hunt Begins

Chapter 2

———— ✦•◆•◆•✦ ————

The Hunting Party followed the road back to where the stagecoach was stopped, and Prince Vaspian was kidnapped,Fretemma who is the tracker of the Party, found many footprints that started where the coach stopped, and they went into the forest.

Frateema counted about six men, and the seventh man would be the Prince. The Party walked half a day before they ran across the small town of Argon.

Frateema told the Hunting Party to stop and stand still, don't make any sudden moves. Then Fratemma told the Party to put down their weapons in front of them., then take a step back, show no hostility. There was an owlbear behind the trees. He means no harm, but will fight if need be. The Owlbear came forth and asked Frateema who could understand all of nature, why were they in the forest?. Frateema told the Owlbear that not more than two days ago six bandits stopped a stagecoach and kidnapped Prince Vaspian, who was on his way to Castle Dragonshire to meet his bride Princess Galanthria.

The Owlbear told Frateema that he saw six men, and a man dressed in robes running deep into the woods, and it looked like the man dressed in robes was not there of his own free will.

The Owlbear told Frateema that her and her men may pick up their arms, and may pass. The Owlbear also said that if there was ever a time that the Party needed help, all Frateema had to do was call him by name, and he would be there. He said his name was Beramus. Deeper into the forest the Party found a small clearing, so they decided to bed down for the night. Kendelyn made a fire, then some coffee, the others unwrapped their bed rolls and placed them close to the fire to keep warm all night. The Party ate salted pork, beans, and had coffee for dinner. The days were still warm, but there was still a chill in the air at night Maliki had put a protection from magic around the camp, and Kendelyn was on guard for a few hours, then Veronna was to take over.

The next morning everyone got up early, rolled up their bed rolls, put out the fire, and started on their way. The party had walked all day. Then that night they came to the village of Pandora. Pandora was a small village. The town consists of a general store, a small inn, a few cottages, and a few fields for planting. They planted potatoes, oranges, rice and green beans. Some people had cows for milk and meat, chickens and pigs as well.

The party stayed at the inn that night. After they had got their rooms (one for the women and one for the men) they all went down to the restaurant downstairs for a meal. They had steak and mashed potatoes, biscuits with butter and jam, coffee and a fruit pie for dessert. The next day Veronna went to the general store to restock on their rations.

Glendoria walked around the town to see if anyone knew of the seven strangers that had been in town, and if so did they say anything?. One woman told Glendoria that earlier that morning a small number of men did come into the town. One of the men acted very strange. The men (all but one harassed the men of the town, and the men destroyed the crops. Then they went to the general store and just took a bunch of food and clothes, beat up the store owner, then left the town.

Once the Hunting Party all got together, Glendoria told the Party what had happened, and that only a few hours ago they had left. Glendoria also told the Party of the damage that the men had done to the crops.

Chapter 3

---·•◆•◆•◆•·---

The party gathered their belongings and went into the forest in the direction that the bandits took the Prince. About four hours into the day's quest, the Party had come across a chromatic (blue) dragon.

Maliki immediately threw a lightning bolt at the blue dragon, but it did not do a thing because the blue dragon is immune to electricity. The blue dragon blew it's fire breath at Veronna, but Veronna held up her shield, and the dragon's breath just went around it.

Arigwin teleported in front of the blue dragon, and at the time she teleported Homri also teleported behind the blue dragon, and they both cast a freezing spell at the same time, and froze the blue dragon on the spot. Then Glendorria walked up and threw her dagger at the dragon's heart, and pierced it right through the center. The dragon's fire heated up the dragon from the inside out and he reached up and took out the dagger, but it was too late the dagger had pierced the dragon's heart to deep, and the dragon fell onto the ground, so Kendelyn went up to the dragon and slit its throat. That night the Party was very tired from their encounter with the dragon, so they found a cool, dry, spot to make camp for the night. Maliki cast a detect magic spell around camp, but he detected something just outside of the camp. A werebear was hiding behind a tree. The werebear changed into a human male and talked to Frateema. The Wearbear said he thought the Hunting Party was made of good people, so he would not fight them, but he was wondering why they were in the forest. Frateema told the werebear that they were sent on a very special quest by King Zandor. Prince Vaspian had been kidnapped as he was on his way to Castle Dragonshire to marry his betrothed, Princess Glanthria. The Party was sent to find him and bring him back alive to marry the Princess..

The werebear said he and his kin were simple creatures, and wish to harm no one, but if forced to they will fight, but only to the point of stopping someone or something. The werebear also said that not more than half a day before the Party had come through a group of men had come through with another man who acted very strange, like he was not part of the group. The werebear thanked Frateema for not harming him, and gave the Party one hundred gold pieces.

The werebear said the men never said where they were going, but that they were heading south. Frateema thanked the werebear for the information, and said that they would be leaving in a couple of hours after they have rested and renewed their strength.

A few hours later they gathered their bedrolls and rations, put out the fire, and headed out into the forest. Then they started to head south again just like the werebear had said.

Chapter 4

—————✦•◆•✦—————

The Party left that morning heading towards the lake There was a long bridge that extended from one side of the lake to the other, the Party started to cross the bridge, but out of a cave next to the bridge came a Cave Troll. The Cave Troll was huffing and puffing, as he stood on one side of the bridge. In a loud, stern, voice the Troll shouted "you cannot cross this bridge".

The troll picked up a large boulder and threw it at the Hunting Party, and almost hit Frateema. Under the bridge there was nothing but bubbling, steaming hot green ooze.

Then Homri ran in front of Frateema, and cast a Flesh to stone spell Cave Troll. The Troll tried to run towards the Party, but the Troll had turned into stone.

After the Troll had turned to stone, Veronna ran up to the Troll and jabbed his sword into the heart of the Troll and broke him into thousands of pieces. A second Cave Troll came out and stomped onto the bridge and yelled at the Hunting Party' You cannot cross this bridge". The Troll started running towards the Hunting Party, and Arigwin cast a water spell on the bridge in front of the Troll, and a large pool of water started to form in front of the Troll. Then out of the pool came Fandoria with her two water dragons. Kendelyn then drew his sword, and started to fight with the Troll Trying to Keep the Troll occupied, while Fandoria told her two dragons the word whind, and the two dragons wrapped around the legs of the Troll. The Troll then tripped over his own feet, and landed hard on the bridge. Glendora then ran up to the Troll and tried to stab him, but the Troll grabbed Glendora. Now Maliki ran up to the Troll, and cut off the Troll's fingers, freeing Glendora. Glendora then twisted her body and sliced open the Troll's throat, killing the Troll instantly.

Now the Hunting Party could cross the bridge.

Chapter 5

The hunting Party traveled for the next few days without running into anything or anyone, so that night the Party decided to make camp. Kendelyn made a fire and made coffee, Veronna went on the hunt for a wild rabbit, or game bird. The party ate good that night. They had rabbit and rice with sage in it, and coffee. Arigwin was on watch that night.

The next day bright and early the Party rolled up their bed rolls, and gathered their things and started back on their way through the forest. The Party traveled for about half a day, and they happened across a group of Dwarves.

There was an elder Dwarf, and eleven younger Dwarves. The elder dwarf stepped up to Frateema and asked her who was in charge, and she said I am kind sir. The elder Dwarf said "alas, you had lost one of your party did you not?". Frateema said, "with a heavy heart I must confess that we did" The elder Dwarf said, "the reason I know this is because he was a part of my kin.

My clan. Frateema said, "yes I know, and I am very sorry. Thank you." the elder Dwarf said. This is why we are here. We want to offer you the services of one of our best fighters. His name is Loren. Loren is one of Gromic's brothers.

Frateema said, "yes, we would be honored to have Loren fighting alongside of us."

Then Frateema asked the elder Dwarf if they had seen a group of men with a hostage come through. These men numbered six, plus one. The one man was dressed in robes that was taken hostage. Even if the men disrobed him, he would be acting like he was not part of the men. The elder Dwarf said, "We overheard some men saying that there was an underground city near here where they were taking their captive, they said that the people there wanted to stone the man for crimes against them. The elder Dwarf said, "head towards the rising sun, and you will come to a cave which is guarded by a red dragon. This is the entrance to the underground city.

The Cave Entrance
To Darkfalls

Chapter 6

————◆•◆•◆————

The party did as the Dwarves said, and walked towards the sunset, and found the cave entrance to Darkfalls, and there was a very large adult Red Dragon guarding the entrance.

Fortunately the Party had the element of surprise, and had the first attack. When the Red dragon fights, he fights inside the cave, never leaving the cave at all.

The Hunting Party slowly, and very quietly moved closer to the cave. As the Red Dragon stood up Maliki noticed that the floor of the cave was sparkling. Red Dragons are known for collecting all kinds of treasure, and magical items such as rings, or weapons, gems, even potions, even gold, silver, or copper.

The Red Dragon can speak human. It said" I can smell human flesh. No one is allowed to enter my cave unless I say they can", but who would be presumptuous enough, or bold enough to enter my cave without my permission?. Since it was night and dark outside, the Hunting Party thought that they could move in without detection, but they were wrong. The Red Dragon had magical spells, so he had detect magic.

He knew just where the Party was at all times. The Dragon used his fire breath, but the Party had strong shields, so they deflected the fire.

Maliki thought that if he could freeze the dragon's heart, he could stab the heart and kill the dragon and break the heart into a hundred pieces.

Maliki cast his freezing spell, but the Dragon's heart was too hot. The freezing spell just melted away. The dragon used his large claws to step on Verona, but he missed. He just scratched her arm with his claw. Then Homri got an idea to freeze the rocks on top of the cave, hoping that they would slide down on top of him. The boulders did fall on top of the dragon knocking him out.

Frateema used her bow and arrows and shot straight into the dragon's heart killing the dragon. The arrow pierced the dragon's heart right in the center.

In the cave the Hunting Party found thirty five gold pieces, sixty silver pieces, a vorpal sword, fifteen rubies, and one hundred emerald pieces.

Of course the party could not carry all of that, and they would not take anymore then they could use.

Arigwin cast a healing spell on Verona's arm which healed 60% of it. Then Homri cast another healing spell on her arm, and healed it the rest of the way.

Chapter 7

Slowly and very carefully the Party made their way into the cave. Homri cast a light spell into the cave from his staff, watching for any pitfalls, traps, or snares that could have been set. The party was even watching for any roaming guards around. The Party was ready for anything.

A few feet into the cave Frateema came across a strange spot in the dirt. The dirt looked like it had been moved. Frateema moved the dirt very carefully with her foot, and sure enough, it was a trap. It was a hole covered with branches with sharp points, so when you fell on them you cut yourself open and bleed to death.

Just before the Hunting Party reached the underground city, the Hunting Party did come across the roaming guards.

Homri did put out his light on his staff so the guards would not see it, but the guard's had detect magic, so they knew where the Hunting Party was.

The guards drew their swords ready to fight. Loren drew his sword and said" I can handle the guards. The guards came at Loren, swinging their swords. Loren swung his sword at one of the guards, and stabbed the guard in the chest killing him. Then he lunged at the other guard slicing the guards throat.

The Hunting Party finally made it to the underground city. The first place the Party saw was the city's Inn. The Party thought they would go to the Inn, one, to see if anyone had heard of the six men and the Prince, and two, because they needed to eat, and rest.

When the party had got to the Inn they had got their rooms. Then they went down to the restaurant to have a good meal. The party had fried chicken, mashed potatoes, biscuits with butter and jam, carrots, and elven wine to drink.

While they were eating, two thieves walked in and plopped down at a table. One of them said" Barkeep, bring us some ale".

The two thieves started talking about the Prince, and how they were going to hang the Prince for the crimes against the people of Englewood. The men said that the Prince had no right to throw the people out of the town just because they were the thieves. The two men kept ordering drinks, and they were getting very drunk. It seemed the more they drank, the more they talked.

Finally the men ran out of money, and Loren shouted" come drink with us"! The Party wanted to get the two men so drunk that they would give them more information on the Prince, and where they were taking him.

The men told the party that the Prince was being kept in a small cottage in the center of town. The men said that in Englewood there was a Mage Guild, and some of the people wanted to start a thieves guild, but the Prince would not allow a thieves guild in his city.

Finally Kendelyn told the men that they had a hard day and were very tired, so the Party headed up to their rooms. The two men were so drunk that the barmaid told them that they could stay in the room in the back of the bar, or so she thought.

Later that night the two men left the Inn and headed back to the shack where the Prince was being held.

While the Hunting Party was at dinner, the barmaid overheard the Party Talking about trying to save the Prince, so when the men had left, the barmaid ran upstairs and told Fratemma that the men had left.

Frateema went and woke up the rest of the party, and told them what had happened. The Party had gotten their things together and went after the two men hoping that they would lead them to the Prince.

Chapter 8

The two thieves were back at the shack. They knew that the Party was out looking for the Prince. The men had the element of surprise and could see when the Hunting Party got there. One of the men Guarding the Prince was a wizard, so he cast a magic missile on the party, but Kendelyn cast detect magic, so they knew that a spell was cast, Homri cast a misdirect spell on the magic missile, and the spell missed the Party. Kendelyn then cast a blindness on the wizard in their group, so he could not see where to cast his spells. The ranger in their group charged Glendora, and hit her in the leg with his sword slicing Glendora's leg open. Arigwin immediately cast a healing spell on Glendora healing her leg. Another one of the guards was also a ranger, and used a bow and arrow. He shot an arrow at Maliki, and hit him in the shoulder. Malki told Kendelyn not to worry about him, but to get the men. Veronna used her bow and arrow and shot at one of the guards, hitting him directly in the heart.

Arigwin cast a sleeping sell on the rest of the group, and they all fell to the ground asleep. Glendoria then walked up and slit all their throats.

There were only two members left in their party that were not affected by the sleeping spell. The two men thought that their lives would be lost if they fought the Hunting Party, so they both just up and ran away.

Homri cast a detect magic on the cottage just in case it was bobitrapped, and in case another group of men came back.

Loren slowly opened the cottage door to see if anyone else was on guard. Inside the shack, the Party located Prince Vaspian. Homri cast a simple unlock spell upon the chains that held the Prince, gave him some water, and some rations, and again slowly opened the door of the cottage and took the Prince out and told him that they were hired by King Zandor to find him and bring the Prince back to Castle Dragonshire.

Going Home

Chapter 9

———————◆◦◆◦◆———————

Now that Prince Vaspian was in the hands of the Hunting Party, and out of the hands of the thieves, in the underground city of Darkfalls, the Hunting Party wanted to keep it that way.

Both the Hunting Party and the Prince made it back to the hotel. They got rooms again and went down to the restaurant for a meal. They all had turkey, potatoes, peas, ale, and fruit pie for dessert.

The next day the Party dressed the Prince up as one of them, so no one would realize who the Prince was. They all had made their way to the cave entrance. Once inside the first thing they confronted was a cave Troll. Cave Trolls are naturally blinded by any light, so Homri casts a spell of light from his staff. The cave Trolls weapon is a club, so since the Troll was blinded, the Troll stood just swinging his club at the Party Arigwin cast a freeze spell on the Troll. Then Homri cast a shatter spell on the Troll, and the Troll shattered into thousands of pieces.

As the party moved on they ran into a cave fisher. The Cave Fisher saw Loren and tried shooting barbs of poison at him, but Loren was able to escape the poison barbs. Homri cast pits and snares, and the cave fisher fell into a pit.

There was a roaming guard on their path, not even realizing there was a cave fisher near. The guard came a bit too close to the cave fisher and the cave fisher shot its poison barbs at him and killed the guard instantly. The barbs had a thread on it thick as a fishing line. The cave Fisher reeled in the strands pulling the guard closer. Once the guard was close enough to the cave Fisher, the Cave Fisher used its pincers to dismember the guard. That way it made it easier to eat the guard. The Cave Fisher forgot all about the Party, so they were able to walk through the cave past the Cave Fisher.

The Hunting Party, and the Prince made it to the exit of the cave and saw the Red Dragon still laying there.

Chapter 10

The Hunting Party pressed on through the forest for a few more miles, and they happened upon a group of twelve mold men. The mold men had the element of surprise, so all of the spells cast from the Hunting Party only had a half strength.

The mold men surrounded the Hunting Party. One of the mold men took one of their spears that they carry and stabbed Kendelyn directly through his back, and straight through his heart. Kendellyn fell right to the ground bleeding profusely. Maliki cast a healing spell on Kendelyn, but it was not strong enough.

Verona used her bow and arrows and shot one of the mold men. She had perfect aim, and hit one of the mold men straight through the heart, and killed him instantly. At the same time that Veronna was attacking the mold men, Kendelyn with his dying breath threw the cloudkill upon the mold men, and it took out four of them.

Glendora threw her two daggers at one of the mold men and killed him. The mold men decided to take the direct approach, and charge the Hunting Party.

The Prince also had learned some spells from his high presets, so Prince Vaspian cast a fire trap at the mold men, and the hairy mold men were set ablaze. Each member of the Hunting Party slit the mold men's throats.

As for Kendelyn, he did not pull through. He had lost too much blood. He had died quickly, without too much pain.

The Hunting Party did find that the mold men did have seven gold pieces, five silver pieces, three rubies, and eight emeralds.

Chapter 11

After the battle, the Hunting party looked for a cool, dry clearing to rest in for the night. They ate some rations, and made a fire for coffee.

The next morning the Party gathered their things, and headed back towards the castle, to the Princess.

The Hunting Party had walked for three days straight, and they did not come across a thing, But on the 4th day they came across a roving band of merchants.

The merchants were just on their way to the next town to see if there was any work. They also said that they just left Castle Dragonshire about a day ago.

Glendora had the Prince's clothes, so Prince Vaspian put back on his robes, so he would look like the Prince again when he got back to the Castle to meet King Zandor, and soon to be bride Glanthria.

The party decided to keep walking. If you do not fight with, or show aggression to merchants, then they will not fight you. The Party was met with a group of the King's Guards. The Party, and the Prince finally arrived at the Castle, and was presented to King Zandor.

King Zandor told Prince Vaspian that later that night the Prince would meet his soon to be bride., and that tomorrow evening they would finally give their hands in marriage to each other.

The night of the Hunting Parties return a dinner was planed in their honor, and to introduce The Prince and the Princess.

At the dinner they had lamb, chicken, and veal. For a vegetable they had peas, green beans, corn on the cob, and beans. For bread they had biscuits, buns, and wheat bread. To drink they had elvine ale, red wine, and white wine. They even had fresh strawberries, and fresh blueberries. The dinner went off without a problem.

For the wedding, the whole kingdom was present. It was held outside in the courtyard.

There were blue flowers everywhere. The bride was in a baby blue dress, long and flowing. The bridesmaids were all dressed in long baby pink dresses. The flowers were white roses.

Now that the Prince of Eagleland, and the Princess of Hollowfield are married, the territory of Eagleland now is an extended land of Hollowfield, protected by Castle Dragonshire.

THE END

A special thanks goes to my husband George Schoff for all of his love, and support. For without George's persistence. I never would have any of my books published.

"The Lord Jesus Christ is my rock, my saviour, and my right hand. For without Jesus, we are nothing."